THE
EARLY
BIRD

GARY RICHMOND

WORD PUBLISHING
Dallas · London · Vancouver · Melbourne

THE EARLY BIRD

Editor: Beverly Phillips

Library of Congress Cataloging-in-Publications Data

Richmond, Gary, 1944–
    The early bird / Gary Richmond ; illustrated by Doug Cushman.
       p.   cm.
    Summary: A little sparrow who tries to fly before he's ready is stranded under a hedge, where he has several scary adventures before he is able to fly away.
    ISBN 0–8499–0924–4
      [1. Sparrows—Fiction. 2. Birds—Fiction. 3. Flight—Fiction.]
  I. Cushman, Doug, ill. II. Title.
  PZ7.R413Ear 1992
  [E]—dc20
                                          92–12326
                                          CIP
                                          AC

Printed in the United States of America

2 3 4 5 6 7 8 9 RRD 9 8 7 6 5 4 3 2 1

To
my favorite aunt
DOROTHY MONTGOMERY
—a constant source of support
and encouragement

"Ouch!" cried Clara.

"Watch out!" said Eunice

"I need more room!" Timothy grumbled.

"I was here first!" complained Muriel.

"This nest is too small," said Nellie.

Timothy Titus Sparrow and his four sisters were exercising their wings. In a few days, when their wings were stronger, they would be ready to fly away from the nest. Until then they practiced by flapping their wings. But in the crowded nest they were beating each other silly.

Timothy was tired of being clobbered by his sisters. He flapped his wings as hard as he could and was able to reach the top edge of the nest.

"Be careful, Timothy," cried Eunice. "You might fall."

"I won't fall," said Timothy. "In fact, I think I can fly now."

"Mom and Dad said to wait," said Muriel, who was the youngest of the five birds.

Timothy Titus paid no attention to their warnings. Instead, he continued to show off. He flapped as hard as he could and surprised everyone by rising above the nest. But Timothy got the biggest surprise of all. He had moved too far away from the nest and didn't have the strength to get back.

"H-E-L-P!" he yelled. But his sisters could do nothing to help him.

Down, down, down went Timothy. The frightened little sparrow landed on the edge of Adelaide Hamilton's yard. Quickly, he jumped under the hedge.

Had Tucker the cat seen him? The big, orange cat belonged to Miss Hamilton. And the sparrows had their nest in a tree next door, high above the roof of Miss Hamilton's beautiful old home.

Like most cats, Tucker liked to eat birds. Timothy and his sisters had seen Tucker from the safety of their nest, and they knew he was dangerous.

Timothy's sisters were crying when their parents returned to the nest. They told their mom and dad what had happened and pointed to where their brother had hidden under the hedge.

"Timothy Titus is an early bird. He was almost ready to leave the nest anyway," their mother said. "I'll feed him on the ground and trust God to protect him until he can fly." Then away she flew.

In no time at all she found Timothy. He looked very ashamed and afraid. She kissed him and told him to stay hidden in the hedge and she would bring him food. If all went well, he would be ready to fly in two more days.

Just before the sun went down, Timothy's mother fed him one more time. She reminded him that he must keep very still. "Cats see movement, but not colors, and God made you to blend in with the leaves and shrubs. So don't move and Tucker won't see you."

Timothy Titus promised he would be very careful. Then he kissed his mother good night, and she flew back to the nest.

Timothy wished he was in the warm nest with his sisters and his mother and father. The strange night sounds were scary by himself. Every footstep, every closing door made him wonder if Tucker were nearby. He stared into the night, shivering with cold and trusted God to take care of him.

At eight o'clock Miss Hamilton opened her front door and let Tucker out. The big, orange cat meowed and slowly headed across the lawn toward the hedge. Timothy's heart beat faster and faster, but he stayed very still, like a statue. Tucker stopped right in front of where Timothy Titus was hiding.

Timothy wanted to scream for help and fly away, but he obeyed his mother and didn't move. Finally, Tucker walked away and disappeared into the night.

The next morning Timothy Titus awoke to the most terrible noise he had ever heard. A man was pushing a lawn mower right at him under the hedge. Timothy flapped his wings as fast as he could. He made it to the sidewalk and landed at the feet of Sam and Angie Cole.

"Look Sam, a little sparrow. We must help him or he'll die."

Sam reached down and gently picked up the little bird. Timothy was shaking. He was afraid Sam and Angie might eat him. The two children took the little sparrow home with them.

Angie got a shoe box and filled it with shredded tissue paper, and Sam gently put Timothy Titus into the box. Poor Timothy didn't know what to think.

"I guess we should feed him some bread and milk," said Sam.

"Mom says we should ask Dr. Sedgwick. He's a veterinarian," Angie said. "He will know what we should do for this little bird."

"I'm glad you came by," said the friendly veterinarian. "That little sparrow probably just wanted to fly before he was ready. Just take him back to where you found him. If you put him under a bush or hedge, the mother sparrow will find him again and feed him. But whatever you do, don't feed him bread and milk. Milk is like poison to birds."

"Will the mother bird still feed him since we have touched him?" Angie wanted to know.

"Yes, Angie. Don't worry about that."

Angie and Sam thanked Dr. Sedgwick and said good-bye. Then they took Timothy Titus back to the hedge close to where they had found him.

Soon Timothy's mother found him, and he told her where he had been. She was surprised the humans had brought him back.

"Timothy Titus," she said, "by tomorrow you should be able to fly. Then you can see your sisters again. They miss you very much."

"I miss them, too," said Timothy.

The day went by very slowly, but Timothy Titus could feel himself getting stronger every hour. Then about two o'clock he met Tuffy James.

Tuffy James was another baby sparrow who also had left the nest a little too early. At first Timothy Titus was glad for the company, but Tuffy was loud and moved around too much. That worried Timothy, and he tried to warn Tuffy about Miss Hamilton's cat. But Tuffy James continued to practice flying.

Just then Tucker noticed movement under the hedge. Timothy Titus froze as soon as he saw Tucker. He tried to whisper to Tuffy, but Tuffy was making too much noise and didn't hear him. Tucker was sneaking close to the ground. And he was headed straight for Timothy's new friend.

Tuffy James turned around just in time to see Tucker coming toward him. "YIKES!" Tuffy yelled and took off. Tucker was gaining on him fast. But Tuffy flew higher. And he managed to make it over a four-foot fence. But Tucker also disappeared over the fence. Timothy Titus prayed that God would help Tuffy get away.

Later, when Timothy's mother came to feed him, he told her what had happened. His mother was very concerned.

"Timothy Titus, it's no longer safe for you on the ground. I want you to fly with me up into that old elm tree in the side yard. I know you can do it Timothy Titus. Just follow me. When I say 'go,' we will run from beneath the hedge and fly up into the tree."

Just then Tucker came home from visiting a cat friend. He saw the two birds, but they didn't see him. Very quietly Tucker began to move toward the mother bird and her young son.

"Go," shouted Timothy's mother, and the two birds began to run. Tucker ran after them. Timothy Titus flapped his wings as hard as he could. Finally, he began to leave the ground. When his mother looked back to see how Timothy was doing, she saw Tucker coming after them.

"Faster," she yelled to her son, and Timothy Titus gave it all he had. He had just begun to rise upward when he felt a terrible jolt and a stinging by his tail feathers. Afraid to look back, Timothy tried even harder. Up, up he flew just like his mother into the high branches of the old elm tree.

On the ground below, Tucker was staring up at them with two tail feathers in his mouth.

Early-bird Timothy Titus had learned to fly just in
time! Soon he would fly away on his own. But first he had
to tell his sisters all about his scary adventures.